Comprehensive Guide On Sexual Fulfilment

Getting the peak of sexual desires

Content

Presentation:

In recent decades, sexual desires and want inconsistency to have gotten even more regularly concentrated as have potential

pharmaceutical intercessions to treat low sexual desire. In any case, the complexities of sexual want including what precisely

is wanted remain inadequately comprehended.

To comprehend the object of people's sexual want, assess sex contrasts and likenesses in the object of want, and look at the effect

of object of want inconsistencies on generally speaking want for accomplice in people with regards to long haul connections

Reports of the object of sexual want notwithstanding proportions of sexual want for current accomplice were gathered from the

two individuals from the couple.

There were huge sex contrasts in the object of sexual want. Men were essentially bound to support want for sexual discharge, climax, and satisfying their accomplice than were ladies. Ladies were essentially bound to underwrite want for closeness, passionate closeness, love, and feeling explicitly attractive than men. Disparities inside the couple as to question of want were identified with their degree of sexual want for accomplice, representing 17% of fluctuation in men's longing and 37% of difference in ladies' craving.

This writeup gives experiences into the conceptualization of sexual want in long haul connections and the multifaceted idea of sexual want that may help in increasingly engaged manners to keep up want over long haul connections. Future research on the utility of this point of view of sexual want and suggestions for clinicians working with couples battling with low sexual want in their connections is talked about.

Definition Of Sex

"Sex" alludes to physiological contrasts found among male, female, and different intersex bodies. Sex incorporates both essential sex qualities (those identified with the conceptive framework) and auxiliary sex attributes (those that are not straightforwardly identified with the regenerative framework, for example, bosoms and facial hair). In people, the organic sex of a kid is resolved during childbirth dependent on a few elements, including chromosomes, gonads, hormones, inside conceptive life structures, and genitalia. Natural sex has generally been conceptualized as a parallel in Western medication, ordinarily isolated into male and female. Notwithstanding, somewhere in the range of 1.0 to 1.7% of youngsters are conceived intersex, having a variety in sex qualities (counting chromosomes, gonads, or private parts) that don't permit them to be particularly distinguished as male or female. Because of the presence of numerous types of intersex conditions (which are more predominant than analysts once suspected), many view sex as existing along a range, as opposed to just two totally unrelated classifications.

Male, female, and the range of sex: In people, sex is commonly partitioned into male, female, or intersex (i.e., having a mix of male and female sex qualities). The above images speak to female on the left and male on the right.

Sexual orientation

An individual's sex, as controlled by their science, doesn't generally compare with their sex; accordingly, the expressions "sex" and "sexual orientation" are not tradable. "Sex" is a term that alludes to social or social qualifications related with being male, female, or intersex. Normally, pampers brought into the world with male sex attributes (sex) are doled out as young men (sexual orientation); babies brought into the world with female sex qualities (sex) are appointed as young ladies (sex). Since our general public works in a paired framework with regards to sexual orientation (at the end of the day, considering sex to be just having two choices), numerous youngsters who are conceived intersex are persuasively alloted as either a kid or a young lady and even carefully "rectified" to fit a specific sex.

Researchers for the most part see sexual orientation as a social build—implying that it doesn't exist normally yet is rather an idea that is made by social and cultural standards.

Sex character is an individual's feeling of self as an individual from a specific sexual orientation. People who relate to a job that compares to the sex alloted to them during childbirth (for instance, they were brought into the world with male sex qualities, were appointed as a kid, and

distinguish today as a kid or man) are cisgender. The individuals who relate to a job that is not quite the same as their natural sex (for instance, they were brought into the world with male sex attributes, were doled out as a kid, yet recognize today as a young lady, lady, or some other sexual orientation through and through) are regularly alluded to as transgender. The expression "transgender" incorporates a wide scope of potential characters, including agender, genderfluid, genderqueer, two-soul (for some indigenous individuals), male/female, and numerous others.

The continuum of sex and sexual orientation: Those who relate to a sex that is unique in relation to their organic sex are called transgender.

Social Variations of Gender

Since the expression "sex" alludes to natural or physical qualifications, attributes of sex won't fluctuate fundamentally between various human social orders. For instance, people of the female sex, when all is said in done, paying little heed to culture, will in the long run bleed and create bosoms that can lactate. Attributes of sex, then again, may change incredibly between various social orders. For instance, in American culture, it is viewed as ladylike (or a characteristic of the female sexual orientation) to wear a dress or skirt. Be that as it may, in many Middle Eastern, Asian, and African societies, dresses or skirts (frequently alluded to as sarongs, robes, or outfits) can be viewed as manly. Essentially, the kilt worn by a Scottish male doesn't cause him to seem female in his way of life.

Sexuality

"Human sexuality" alludes to individuals'
sexual enthusiasm for and fascination in
others, just as their ability to have sensual
encounters and reactions. Individuals' sexual
direction is their passionate and sexual
appreciation for specific genders or sexes,
which regularly shapes their sexuality.
Sexuality might be experienced and
communicated in an assortment of ways,
including contemplations, dreams, wants,
convictions, perspectives, values, practices,
practices, jobs, and connections. These may
show themselves in organic, physical,
passionate, social, or otherworldly
perspectives. The natural and physical parts
of sexuality to a great extent concern the
human conceptive capacities, including the
human sexual-reaction cycle and the
essential organic drive that exists in all
species. Enthusiastic parts of sexuality
incorporate securities between people that
are communicated through significant
emotions or physical appearances of
adoration, trust, and care. Social
perspectives manage the impacts of human
culture on one's sexuality, while
otherworldliness concerns a person's
profound association with others through
sexuality. Sexuality additionally impacts and
is affected by social, political, legitimate,

philosophical, good, moral, and strict parts
of life.

The Standard Model of the Terms

The expressions "sex" and "sex" have not
generally been separated in the English
language, and it was not until the 1950s that
they officially started to be recognized. With
an end goal to explain use of the expressions
"sex" and "sexual orientation," preparation,
"The word 'sex' has procured the new and
helpful undertone of social or attitudinal
qualities (instead of physical attributes)
unmistakable to the genders. In other words,
sex is to sex as ladylike is to female and
manly is to male"

The standard model of the contrast among
sex and sexual orientation says that one's sex
is naturally decided (implying that when a
kid is conceived, specialists order the kid as
a specific sex contingent upon life systems),
while one's sex is socially or socially
decided (implying that the manner by which
that kid is raised, mingled, and instructed

decides if they take on manly or female characteristics). The standard model has been scrutinized for saying that people are explicitly dimorphic: this implies every single individual is either male or female, consequently forgetting about the individuals who are conceived intersex. The standard model clarifies that sexual orientation is classified into two independent, rival sides, being either manly or ladylike, again totally barring the individuals who are intersex, transgender, male/female, etc.

What Is Desire?

Want is truly the inclination that goes with an unsatisfied state." Desire can prompt new and better things; it can likewise get us in a tough situation. It is the catalyst for pretty much everything; want is probability.

Normally, we will in general consider want a feeling — that is, emerging from our psychological status, much the same as love or outrage or melancholy or shock or joy.

However, this is likely not the situation. Numerous researchers and therapists presently accept that craving is, truth be told, a real urge, progressively closely resembling hunger or the blood's requirement for oxygen. For any individual who has been maddeningly infatuated, headed to the edge of hopelessness by an insatiable want for another, this likely doesn't appear to be so fantastical. from numerous points of view we can't control what we want since it is a hard-wired enthusiastic and physiological reaction. - sexual want.

Nothing unexpected: want and sexuality are essentially inseparable. "Desire" likely infers brownish romance books, grown-up just exercises, and a yearning for sexual association.

Sexual want may in certainty be the main sort of want; psychoanalytic hypothesis holds that every other type of want and innovative vitality are the aftereffect of rerouted sexual vitality — frequently called "the moxie" — towards different undertakings.

The substantial inclination of want is just sexual in nature; everything else is a passionate state created out of this essential want.

Regardless of whether you purchase that, plainly sexual want is one of the — if not the — most grounded of human needs. Commonly, it takes up a colossal segment within recent memory, enthusiastic vitality, and lives. Why? What drives the frequently relentless cargo train of sexual want?

Arrangement of Desire

Want is the meeting up of visual,
biochemical, enthusiastic, and
biomechanical signals that trigger a
hormonal course that may finish in the
fruitful preparation of an egg by a sperm. A
really clinical clarification, yet one held
generally all through the calling and related
fields of study.

The inclinations we have in our sexual lives
are, pretty much, basically a statement of
our quest for transformative bit of leeway.

Want is without a doubt dependent on a
developmental need, we have an
exceptionally solid, once in a while
oblivious want to propagate our species.

Sustaining humanity is oblivious. The
outflow of sexual want — our cognizant
emotions and our exhibitions of sexuality —
is definitely more perplexing than simply
attempting to have babies.

The outflow of sexual want is undoubtedly established in youth. youngsters watch their folks and retain exercises about parental sexuality and want. Even though from the start we do not have the capacity or the event to communicate them, these underlying impressions of want are not lost on us. At the point when we enter adolescence, we begin to feel the transformative want towards generation.

Quickly, this craving starts to communicate as the educated sexuality we have been absorbing since adolescence.

As we develop more seasoned, it changes as it is formed by meaningful gestures from our companions and by broad communications depictions. It might take one of any number of structures; however want might be straightforward, sexuality is diverse and changed. Sexuality is the statement of want, and the part of want we can get to, control, and appreciate.

Secrets of Desire

At the point when the innovation to take a gander at mind movement during sexual incitement opened up, researchers anticipated that it should show a genuinely straight way from visual acknowledgment to enthusiastic/sexual intrigue. But then the mind imaging indicated that sexual want makes an extraordinarily perplexing and non-direct system of cerebrum movement, remembering illuminating areas for the mind ordinarily gave to "higher" capacities, for example, mindfulness and getting others, preceding illuminating the more clear physical-reaction segments. Everything happens unfathomably quick and frequently underneath the radar of awareness. By and large, individuals don't appear to realize what turns them on.

Logical clarification of want show that the cooperation of neuro-synthetic substances associated with want is thick and tangled. What's more, the mechanics of what may end up being the most basic component of want - phermones and cranial nerve zero - still stays muddled.

The entirety of this disarray helps to clarify why treatment techniques for loss of charisma appear, best case scenario aimless and frequently insufficient. By and large, fake treatments will in general work similarly just as the genuine article. [If you're intrigued, truly, Viagra works, yet it doesn't really influence want; it influences excitement, a totally extraordinary substantial component (and an entire other discussion)].

Possibly the disarray is not so terrible. What is pleasant about the failure of science to completely disentangle this riddle is that it keeps a portion of the enchantment of adoration and want alive. All things considered, if want was a thing known, maybe it would never again be a thing to prop us up. Maybe without the vulnerability, we would not have had Adam and Eve, or the Sorrows of Young Werther, or Titanic. So maybe it is best not to know all things considered.

Sexual Desire

Sexual desire is an inspirational state and an enthusiasm for sexual articles or exercises, or as a desire, or drive to search out sexual items or to participate in sexual exercises. Equivalents for sexual want are charisma, sexual fascination and desire.

Sexual want is a part of an individual's sexuality, which differs fundamentally starting with one individual then onto the next, and furthermore fluctuates relying upon conditions at a specific time. Few out of every odd individual encounter sexual want; the individuals who don't encounter it might be named agamic.

Sexual want might be the "absolute most regular sexual occasion in the lives of people". Sexual want is an emotional inclination express that can "be activated by both inward and outside prompts, and that could conceivably bring about obvious sexual conduct.

Sexual want can be stimulated through creative mind and sexual dreams or seeing a person whom one finds appealing. Sexual want is likewise made and enhanced through sexual strain, which is brought about by sexual want that still can't seem to be culminated.

Sexual want can be unconstrained or responsive. Sexual want is dynamic, can either be sure or contrary, and can fluctuate in power contingent upon the ideal article or individual.

The creation and utilization of sexual dream and thought is a significant piece of appropriately working sexual want. Some physical indications of sexual want in people are; licking, sucking, puckering and contacting the lips, just as tongue distension.

Hypothetical viewpoints

Scholars and specialists have normally utilized two distinct systems in their comprehension of human sexual want. The first is an organic system where sexual want originates from an inborn persuasive power like "a sense, drive, need, urge, wish, or need". Otherwise called sex drive.

Second, a socio-social hypothesis where want is conceptualized as one factor in an a lot bigger setting (for example connections settled inside social orders, settled inside societies).

In the organic methodology, sexual drive is compared to other natural drives, for example, hunger, where an individual will search out food, or on account of want – joy, to lessen or keep away from torment.

Sex drive can be thought of as a natural need or desiring that motivates people to search out and get responsive to sexual encounters and sexual delight. Be that as it may, individuals from all species (counting people) won't look to take part in sexual movement with any con-explicit, since fascination assumes an enormous job in sexual want.

Motivator inspiration hypothesis exists under this system. This hypothesis expresses that the quality of inspiration towards sexual movement relies upon the quality of the upgrades (promptness of boosts), and if satiety is accomplished, the quality of the improvements/impetus will be expanded later.

Sex drive is rigidly attached to natural factors, for example, "chromosomal and hormonal status, wholesome status, age, and general wellbeing".

Sexual desire is the main period of the human sex reaction cycle. The conventional model for the human sexual reaction cycle can be spoken to as: **Desire** → **Arousal** → **Orgasm** → **Resolution**.

Sexual want, however, a piece of the sexual reaction cycle, is accepted to be unmistakable and separate from genital sexual excitement. It has likewise been contended that sexual want is certifiably not a stage in sexual reaction. Or maybe, it is something that continues through excitement and climax and can even persevere after climax.

Despite the fact that climax may make it hard for a man to keep up his erection or lady proceed with vaginal oil, sexual want can endure all things considered.

In the socio-social system, sexual want would demonstrate a yearning for the good of sexual action for its own, not for some other reason than only for pleasure and one's own fulfilment or to discharge some sexual pressure.

Sexual want and action could likewise be created to help accomplish some different methods or to increase some different prizes that may not be sexual in starting point, as expanded closeness and connection between accomplices. Sexual want isn't a urge; this may suggest that people have to a greater degree their very own cognizant control want.

That being stated, socio-social impacts may drive guys and females into sexual orientation explicit jobs where the utilization of social contents directing the proper sentiments and reactions to want and movement are normal. This may prompt clash where a person's needs might be unfulfilled because of the foreseen social results of their activities, causing dissatisfaction.

A few scholars recommend that the experience of sexual want might be socially built. In any case, some contend that in spite of the fact that socio-social components are exceptionally persuasive over the experience of sexual want, they don't assume a huge job until after organic at first impacts want.

Another view is that sexual want is neither a social development nor a natural drive. As per James Giles, it is somewhat an existential need that depends on the feeling of deficiency that emerges from the experience of being gendered.

There are numerous scientists who accept that focusing on any single way to deal with the investigation of human sexuality and barring others is not legitimate and counterproductive.

It is the reconciliations of and association between different methodologies and orders that will permit us the most exhaustive comprehension of human sexuality from all points. One single methodology may give essential variables to contemplating want, yet it isn't adequate. Sexual want can show itself in more than one way; it is a "wide range of conduct, cognition's, and feelings, taken together".

Sexual want has three parts which connect a few distinctive hypothetical points of view together:

Drive – The natural part. This incorporates life systems and neuroendocrine physiology.

Inspiration – The mental segment. This incorporates the impacts of individual mental states (temperament), relational

states (for example common love,
difference), and social setting (for example
relationship status).

Wish – The social segment. This thinks
about social standards, qualities, and rules
about sexual articulation which are outer to
the person.

Sexual Arousal

Sexual excitement or sexual energy is normally the excitement of sexual want during or fully expecting sexual movement. Various physiological reactions happen in the body and psyche as groundwork for sex and keep during it. Male excitement will prompt an erection, and in female excitement the body's reaction is engorged sexual tissues, for example, areolas, vulva, clitoris, vaginal dividers and vaginal grease. Mental boosts and physical upgrades, for example, contact, and the inner variance of hormones, can impact sexual excitement.

Sexual excitement has a few phases and may not prompt any genuine sexual action, past a psychological excitement and the physiological changes that go with it. Given adequate sexual incitement, sexual excitement in people arrives at its peak during a climax. It might likewise be sought after for the wellbeing of its own, even without a climax.

There are a few in-customs, terms and expressions to portray sexual excitement including horny, turned on, randy, hot, and salacious. Things that hasten human sexual excitement are called suggestive boosts and informally known as turn-ons.

Suggestive improvements

Sexual incitement and Erogenous zone

Contingent upon the circumstance, an individual can be explicitly stimulated by an assortment of components, both physical and mental. An individual might be explicitly excited by someone else or by specific parts of that individual, or by a non-human item. The physical incitement of an erogenous zone or demonstrations of foreplay can bring about excitement, particularly on the off chance that it is went with the expectation of up and coming sexual action. Sexual excitement might be helped by a sentimental setting, music or other mitigating circumstance. The potential boosts for sexual excitement fluctuate from individual to individual, and starting with one time then onto the next, as does the degree of excitement.

Upgrades can be ordered by the sense in question: somatosensory (contact), visual, and olfactory (fragrance).

Sound-related upgrades are additionally conceivable, however they are commonly viewed as auxiliary in job to the next three.[citation needed] Erotic boosts which can bring about sexual excitement can incorporate discussion, perusing, movies or pictures, or a smell or setting, any of which can produce sensual considerations and recollections in an individual.

Given the correct setting, these may prompt the individual craving physical contact, including kissing, nestling, and petting of an erogenous zone. This may thus make the individual want direct sexual incitement of the bosoms, areolas, bottom as well as private parts, and further sexual movement.

Suggestive improvements may begin from a source disconnected to the object of ensuing sexual intrigue. For instance, numerous individuals may discover nakedness, erotica or sex entertainment explicitly stirring. This may create a general sexual intrigue that is

fulfilled by sexual movement. At the point
when sexual excitement is accomplished by
or reliant on the utilization of items, it is
alluded to as sexual fetishism, or in certain
cases a paraphilia.

Analysts read the time required for a person
to arrive at the pinnacle of sexual excitement
while observing explicitly express motion
pictures or pictures and reached the
resolution that on normal ladies and men set
aside nearly a similar effort for sexual
excitement —

around 10 minutes. The time required for
foreplay is exceptionally individualistic and
shifts starting with one time then onto the
next relying upon numerous conditions.

In contrast to numerous different creatures,
people do not have a mating season, and

both genders are conceivably equipped for sexual excitement consistently.

Sexual excitement for a great many people is a constructive encounter and a part of their sexuality and is frequently looked for.

An individual can typically control how they will react to excitement. They will typically comprehend what things or circumstances are conceivably animating and may at their relaxation choose to either make or maintain a strategic distance from these circumstances. Additionally, an individual's sexual accomplice will ordinarily likewise know their accomplice's suggestive upgrades and mood killers.

A few people feel humiliated by sexual excitement and some are explicitly hindered. A few people do not feel excited on each event that they are presented to sensual upgrades, nor act in a sexual path on each excitement. An individual can take a functioning part in a sexual movement without sexual excitement. These circumstances are viewed as typical, yet rely upon the development, age, culture and different variables affecting the individual.

In any case, when an individual neglects to be stimulated in a circumstance that would consistently deliver excitement and the absence of excitement is industrious, it might be because of a sexual excitement issue or hypoactive sexual want issue.

There are numerous reasons why an individual neglects to be stimulated, including a psychological issue, for example, despondency, sedate use, or a clinical or state of being. The absence of sexual excitement might be because of a general absence of sexual want or because of an absence of sexual want for the present accomplice.

An individual may consistently have had no or low sexual want or the absence of want may have been procured during the individual's life. There are likewise intricate philosophical and mental issues encompassing sexuality. Mentalities towards life, passing, labor, one's folks, companions, family, contemporary society, mankind as a rule, and especially one's place on the planet assume a considerable job in deciding how an individual will react in some random sexual circumstance.

Then again, an individual might be hypersexual, which is a craving to take part in sexual exercises thought about anomalous high comparable to ordinary turn of events or culture, or experiencing a diligent genital excitement issue, which is an unconstrained, tenacious, and wild excitement, and the physiological changes related with excitement.

Physiological reactions

Sexual excitement causes different physical reactions, most fundamentally in the sex organs (genital organs). Sexual excitement for a man is generally demonstrated by the growing and erection of the penis when blood fills the corpus cavernosum. This is generally the most conspicuous and solid indication of sexual excitement in guys. In a lady, sexual excitement prompts expanded

blood stream to the clitoris and vulva, just as
vaginal transudation - the leaking of
dampness through the vaginal dividers
which fills in as oil.

Male Sexual Arousal

It is entirely expected to correspond the erection of the penis with male sexual excitement. Physical or mental incitement, or both, prompts vasodilation and the expanded blood stream engorges the three light regions that run along the length of the penis (the two corpora cavernosa and the corpus spongiosum). The penis becomes augmented and firm, the skin of the scrotum is pulled more tightly, and the testicles are pulled facing the body.

In any case, the connection among erection and excitement isn't balanced. After their mid-forties, a few men report that they don't generally have an erection when they are explicitly excited. Similarly, a male erection can happen during rest (nighttime penile bloat) without cognizant sexual excitement or because of mechanical incitement (for example scouring against the bed sheet) alone.

A youngster — or one with a solid charisma
— may encounter enough sexual excitement
for an erection to result from a passing idea,
or simply seeing a bystander. When erect,
his penis may increase enough incitement
from contact with within his garments to
keep up and energize it for quite a while.

As sexual excitement and incitement
proceeds, almost certainly, the glans or
leader of the erect penis will expand more
extensive and, as the private parts become
additionally engorged with blood, their
shading develops and the gonads can grow
up to half bigger.

As the balls keep on rising, a sentiment of
warmth may create around them and the
perineum. With further sexual incitement,
the pulse builds, circulatory strain rises and
breathing turns out to be speedier. The
expansion in blood stream in the genital and
different districts may prompt a sex flush
here and there, in certain men.

As sexual incitement proceeds, climax starts, when the muscles of the pelvic floor, the vas deferens (between the balls and the prostate), the original vesicles and the prostate organ itself may start to contract such that powers sperm and semen into the urethra inside the penis. When this has begun, all things considered, the man will proceed to discharge and climax completely, with or moving along without any more incitement.

Similarly, if sexual incitement stops before climax, the physical impacts of the incitement, including the vasocongestion, will die down in a brief timeframe. Rehashed or drawn out incitement without climax and discharge can prompt distress in the testicles (relating to the slang term "blue balls".

After climax and discharge, men for the most part experience an unmanageable period portrayed by loss of erection, a subsidence in any sex flush, less enthusiasm for sex, and a sentiment of unwinding that can be ascribed to the neurohormones oxytocin and prolactin.

The force and length of the obstinate period can be short in an exceptionally stimulated youngster in what he sees as a profoundly exciting circumstance, maybe without even an observable loss of erection. It very well may be up to a couple of hours or days in midlife and older men.

The connection between sexual want and excitement in men is unpredictable, with a wide scope of components expanding or diminishing sexual excitement.

Physiological reactions, for example, pulse, circulatory strain, and erection, are frequently harsh with self-revealed emotional view of excitement. This irregularity recommends that mental or intellectual angles likewise strongly affect sexual excitement.

The psychological parts of sexual excitement in men are not totally known, yet the state involves the examination and assessment of the upgrade, arrangement of the boost as sexual, and a full of feeling reaction.

Research proposes that psychological elements, for example, sexual inspiration, saw sex job desires, and sexual perspectives, add to sex contrasts saw in emotional sexual excitement. In particular, while watching hetero sensual recordings, men are more impacted by the sex of the entertainers depicted in the improvement, and men might be more probable than ladies to externalize the on-screen characters.

There are accounted for contrasts in cerebrum enactment to sexual improvements, with men indicating more significant levels of amygdala and hypothalamic reactions than ladies. This proposes the amygdala assumes a basic job in the handling of explicitly exciting visual boosts in men.

Female Sexual Arousal

The beginnings of sexual excitement in a lady's body is normally set apart by vaginal grease (wetness; however this can happen without excitement because of contamination or cervical bodily fluid creation around ovulation), expanding and engorgement of the outer privates, and inward extending and amplification of the vagina.

There have been studies to discover the level of connection between these physiological reactions and the lady's emotional vibe of being explicitly stirred: the discoveries for the most part are that at times there is a high relationship, while in others, it is shockingly low.

Further incitement can prompt further vaginal wetness and further engorgement and expanding of the clitoris and the labia, alongside expanded redness or obscuring of the skin in these regions as blood stream increments. Further changes to the inward organs additionally happen including to the inner state of the vagina and to the situation of the uterus inside the pelvis.

Different changes remember an expansion for pulse just as in circulatory strain, feeling hot and flushed and maybe encountering tremors. A sex flush may reach out over the chest and chest area.

On the off chance that sexual incitement proceeds, at that point sexual excitement may top into climax. After climax, a few ladies don't need any further incitement and the sexual excitement rapidly disperses.

Proposals have been distributed for proceeding with the sexual fervor and moving from one climax into further incitement and keeping up or recapturing a condition of sexual excitement that can prompt second and ensuing climaxes. A few ladies have encountered such different climaxes unexpectedly.

While young ladies may turn out to be explicitly stirred effectively, and arrive at climax moderately rapidly with the correct incitement in the correct conditions, there are physical and mental changes to ladies' sexual excitement and reactions as they age.

More seasoned ladies produce less vaginal oil and studies have explored changes to degrees of fulfilment, recurrence of sexual action, to want, sexual considerations and dreams, sexual excitement, convictions about and mentalities to sex, torment, and the capacity to arrive at climax in ladies in their 40s and after menopause.

Different elements have likewise been examined including socio-segment factors, wellbeing, mental factors, accomplice factors, for example, their accomplice's wellbeing or sexual issues, and way of life factors. Apparently these different factors regularly greaterly affect ladies' sexual working than their menopausal status.

It is along these lines seen as significant consistently to comprehend the "setting of ladies' lives" when considering their sexuality.

Diminished estrogen levels might be related with expanded vaginal dryness and less clitoral erection when stimulated yet are not legitimately identified with different parts of sexual intrigue or excitement. In more seasoned ladies, diminished pelvic muscle tone may imply that it takes more time for excitement to prompt climax, may decrease the power of climaxes, and afterward cause progressively quick goals. The uterus normally contracts during climax and, with propelling age, those constrictions may really get excruciating.

Research proposes that intellectual variables like sexual inspiration, saw sex job desires, and sexual mentalities assume significant jobs in ladies' self-announced degrees of sexual excitement.

Ladies requirements for closeness prompts them to connect with sexual upgrades, which prompts an encounter of sexual want and mental sexual excitement.

Mental sexual excitement additionally affects physiological systems. Sexual cognizance's effect hormone levels in ladies, to such an extent that sexual musings bring about a quick increment in testosterone in ladies who were not utilizing hormonal contraception.

As far as cerebrum enactment, scientists have proposed that amygdala reactions are not exclusively controlled by level of self-detailed sexual excitement, ladies self-revealed higher sexual excitement than men, however experienced lower levels of amygdala reactions.

Sexual excitement in ladies is portrayed by vasocongestion of the genital tissues, including inward and outside territories (e.g., vaginal dividers, clitoris, and labia). There are an assortment of techniques used to survey genital sexual excitement in ladies.

Vaginal photoplethysmography (VPG) can gauge changes in vaginal blood volume or phasic changes in vasocongestion related with every heartbeat.

Clitoral photoplethysmography works along these lines to VPG, yet gauges changes in clitoral blood volume, instead of vaginal vasocongestion. Thermography gives an immediate proportion of genital sexual excitement by estimating changes in temperature related with expanded blood stream to the outside genital tissues.

Likewise, labial thermistor cuts measure changes in temperature related with genital engorgement; this strategy straightforwardly quantifies changes in temperature of the labia. More as of late, laser doppler imaging (LDI) has been utilized as an immediate proportion of genital sexual excitement in ladies. LDI works by estimating shallow changes in blood stream in the vulvar tissues.

Reasons Most Women Lack Sex-Drive

You used to need to remove your better half's garments. Presently? Not really.

On the off chance that you have been experiencing "sweetheart, not tonight" disorder (a.k.a. low sex drive), wellbeing specialists state you're not the only one. It's assessed that upwards of 40 million ladies in the United States experience the ill effects of a winding down drive. Here are 10 of the most widely recognized—and astonishing—reasons why your sex drive may have taken a crash, and how to get your groove back.

Messy Bedroom -What does your room resemble at this moment? Is the bed unmade? Are your dressers heaped high with books, magazines and residue? Past research has connected room mess with misery and gentle discouragement, yet a few specialists make it a stride further and state that an untidy room could be the reason for a dreary sex drive. We do realize that ladies, more so than men, are inclined to intellectual interruptions—considering other things in manners that meddle with sex.

A chaotic room could increment such intellectual interruptions. It could make you figure 'I should get new window ornaments or Look at that heap of bills—I trust I previously paid the power . "Chaos is a token of the considerable number of things we haven't done at this point.

This can significantly meddle with a feeling of quiet, which can push ladies to unwind, centre only around their sentiments of adoration and want, and at that point get in the state of mind for sex."

Tackle the messiness, and other diverting things in your boudoir. "In the event that you and your accomplice observe an excess of TV, move it to the lounge. On the off chance that there's a pile of mail or bills, put them in a room that you partner with work, not rest or sex.

Outrage -In case you are uncertain why your sex drive has failed recently, think about this amazing source: subdued annoyance. it is probably the greatest reason for low sex drive in ladies. Ladies who have a great deal of sentiments of outrage toward their accomplice—regardless of whether it is disturbance that he didn't help around the house or something else genuine—do not want to have intercourse. Outrage suppresses all longing."

Track down the wellspring of the resentment, and arrangement with it, Whether it's outrage regarding his absence of compassion or the way that he didn't do the dishes the previou evening, don't let outrage become harmful to your relationship."

Compulsiveness - Your better half's in the state of mind, however you're most certainly not. All things considered; how would you be able to be? There's unfurled clothing heaped high on the bed, you just got back from the exercise centre (and have not showered at this point) and the infant is presumably going to wake up for his 9 p.m. taking care of any second. Sound natural?

Hair splitting spots an enormous weight on sex drive.

A stickler thinks she needs to look and smell great, her mate must be great and nature must be great." Here's the issue: "This condition of flawlessness, obviously, is outlandish. Along these lines, the stickler is worried about the defects instead of getting a charge out of time with her accomplice."

The Economy - Would it be able to be conceivable that the downturn has entered… your room? For sure, monetary concerns can affect moxie. Stress can exhaust any sex drive, and it does not need to be about the relationship or sex.

A great deal of people who are stressed over the economy, losing their employments, or not having the option to resign when they had arranged are too whining of having no longing for physical closeness. Research appears stress and stress top the reasons for low sex drive. If you cannot cause your concerns to leave, attempt to understand them at any rate. Rather than lying in bed around evening time pondering how much cash you lost in the stock market or whether you will have the option to make your home instalment, reveal to yourself you're just permitted to stress at specific occasions of the day. Calendar some an opportunity to stress. This may appear to be odd, yet look into shows that doing this will really diminish your stressing."

Physical closeness is an incredible method to battle pressure and stress. So consider sex a type of treatment.

Uncertain Trauma - Was your home broken into a year ago? Did a nearby beyond words as of late? Are you despite everything feeling the impacts of a horrible birth— months, years after the fact? "While injury may have occurred in the past, it can keep on influencing you, and your sex drive.

Truth be told, some psychological wellness experts accept that diminished charisma ought to be a vital symptomatic rule for post-awful pressure issue.

Even however it might have occurred previously, you can deliver your response to the injury. At the point when it makes sense excuse the individual who wronged you. Yet in addition excuse yourself.

Furthermore, do look for proficient help on the off chance that you have to. friends and family merit it.

High Cholesterol - We can connect relationship between elevated cholesterol and ladies who think that its troublesome with excitement

also, climax. Here's the reason: "Cholesterol can develop on the dividers of the supply routes of the body, including those to the pelvic zone.

Scientists theorize that when blood stream to the pelvic region is limited, there can be less sensation in the private parts. That can make climax progressively troublesome, which can thus make sex baffling."

To curb this, simply hange your eating routine! lessening the measure of entire milk items and creature fats you devour while increasing your admission of organic products, vegetables and other fiber-rich

nourishments, which could help obstruct the
assimilation of cholesterol in the circulation
system and improve your sexual wellbeing.

Contraception - Ironically, what should
cause sex to feel more liberating and
agreeable could be what makes your sex
drive flatline, yet it's actual. Hormone-based
conception prevention, expands your sex

hormone restricting globulin, which
diminishes testosterone. That is clinical
represent "there's a decent possibility your
conception prevention pills may be
meddling with your sex drive."

Consider a copper intrauterine gadget for
additional enduring, and without hormone,
anti-conception medication; switch back to
condoms (they're not unreasonably terrible);
or converse with your primary care
physician about changing your solution,
particularly in case you're encountering
vaginal dryness combined with a lack of
engagement in sex.

Keep in mind, the preventative that works for one lady's drive may not for another. "It's distinctive for each lady and relies upon the detailing.

Undiscovered Thyroid Problem - It is just about the size of a golf ball, however your thyroid might be unleashing destruction on your drive. One of the side effects of the underactive thyroid condition known as

hypothyroidism—alongside weight gain, male pattern baldness, dry skin and weariness—is a floundering sex drive.

Make an arrangement to see your primary care physician. A basic blood test can analyse hypothyroidism, which is without any problem treatable with drug.

No Date Nights - on the off chance that you don't have a night out on the town arranged with your spouse and can't recollect the last time you plunked down and associated— regardless of whether it was directly over the kitchen table.

Research has it that ladies with low sex drive regularly have an absence of enthusiastic association with their accomplices.

Plan a night out, obviously! Here is a few schoolwork for the room: couples ought to move away from a presentation-based sexuality, where sex is normally characterized as intercourse and obligatory climaxes yet rather taking up delight based sexuality, where the emphasis is on joy, fun and closeness.

*You are Nursing Mum-*You had your lovable beloved newborn months back and lost (a large portion) of the pregnancy weight, so for what reason hasn't your sex drive returned? In case you are yet nursing, accuse your bosoms.

Things being what they are, prolactin, the hormone that is liable for lactation, is a genuine buzz execute for the drive, diminishing your body's creation of estrogen and testosterone. This can prompt vaginal dryness and absence of sex drive.

First, extol yourself for putting resources into the strength of your infant, and recall that it's just brief. All things considered, you are not going to breastfeed your infant until the end of time! In the interim, use a lot of ointment and make an effort not to feel baffled at your body's gradualness to feel stimulated

How To Keep Your Woman Satisfied in Bed

On the off chance that you are a man who truly needs to satisfy his accomplice in bed, at that point this accomplish more assistance.

It is composed for the individuals who contribute, men that are completely turned on by the idea of fulfilling their accomplice in bed.

It's additionally for men who found out about sexless relationships and need to keep away from it in their relationship. Maybe you even encountered a sexless relationship before and you would prefer not to rehash this situation with your current/future relationship.

It's for you in the event that you are the sort that ensures your accomplice has an climax before you do. You teach yourself about the most ideal approaches to mind for your accomplice during sex.

You ace oral sex, or pussy back rub, or whatever other able method that should shoot firecrackers through your accomplice's spine. There's huge amounts of astonishing

data about how to satisfy your lady in bed
out there.

Your partner will not appreciate any of the
awesome sex deceives you are anticipating
performing except if you spread one thing
first. What you don't comprehend about
ladies and sex.

As a man, your mind turns off during sex
easily. Your lady, be that as it may, isn't
really ready to turn off her mind without any
problem. Indeed, regardless of whether you
utilize the most incredibly sex move that
you came over, ever.

Turning our mind off during sex is
precarious for ladies because of a couple of
reasons. Social moulding is a significant
one.

It may be fine toward the beginning of the
relationship, when sex tends to be
energizing. During the wedding trip period
of the relationship, both people are getting a
charge out of the investigation. Becoming
more acquainted with one another is a

procedure that stretches out into the lovemaking.

Everything is new, and uncovering the new domain of another accomplice is empowering.

Be that as it may, when the fervour begins to blur, old examples develop. This is when, regardless of whether you give a valiant effort to keep your accomplice fulfilled explicitly, things may go pear-melded for her. She may continue doing very similar things, making quite a few moves and quite a few sounds.

She may even now put forth an attempt to satisfy you. However, really, her brain meanders somewhere else.

Our brains are really endeavouring to ensure we're absent since we shouldn't appreciate sex. typically ladies are the ones to convey a subliminal conviction that sex is "filthy", "awful", or "hazardous".

Clearly, a few ladies don't have any of these issues and they keep on getting a charge out of sex effectively and normally.

In any case, the issue is, numerous ladies love sex to begin with, and later on they quit appreciating it. What is more, you (or her) would not know it until it as of now occurs. So it may be justified, despite all the trouble to attempt this one thing to be erring on the side of caution.

Ladies do not comprehend it themselves.

We experienced childhood in a general public that conveys a sexual getting that comes from a male point of view of sexuality.

We think we should react to sexual signals with a certain goal in mind.

It works for (most) men and for certain ladies. Be that as it may, numerous ladies are unsatisfied explicitly on the grounds that they attempt to fit themselves into a sexual model that just does not work for them. What is more, as they were never presented to an alternate worldview, they wind up

being to an ever increasing extent baffled
and finding no alleviation.

Regardless of how astounding your sex
strategies are, regardless of what you do to
ensure she starts things out, it will not help if
your lady is going through the way toward
closing explicitly.

What is more, the most serious issue that
you're confronting, as a caring accomplice
that needs to satisfy his lady, is that, most
likely, she is feeling awkward telling you
what is troubling her. By and large,

ladies feel too humiliated to even consider
admitting — even to themselves — that they
are discontent with their sexual experiences.

So your lady is unsatisfied with her sexual
coexistence, despite the fact that you are still
devoted and go the additional mile to satisfy
her in bed. She does not have the foggiest
idea why. She presumably feels remorseful

without acknowledging it, presently for two reasons:

1. She's feeling regretful for engaging in sexual relations since sex is "filthy";

2. She's feeling regretful for despising it since she realizes you are giving a valiant effort to fulfil her.

Furthermore, if that is the situation for her, regardless of how diligently you attempt to please her explicitly, it aren't going to work.

What is going to work?

To ensure that your drawn out accomplice remains fulfilled explicitly, you should be the facilitator of a change in outlook.

Which change in outlook, you inquire? The one that takes all that you both accept about sex and junks it.

The move changes the accentuation from having an energizing sex life, to a satisfying sexual coexistence.

This kind of sex doesn't have a ultimate objective of an exceptional climax.

Rather, its will probably expand the closeness between you. It is the sort of sex that doesn't connect itself with blame, disgrace, and other awkward sentiments.

The kind of sex that you are not presented to in our general public's regular portrayals of sex.

Careful sex. Careful sex can possibly make the necessary move. Since it's so far expelled from the manner in which we regularly figure sex ought to be — it permits your lady to investigate and acknowledge her actual sexual potential. With no strain to accomplish an objective. Simply be, and interface. that is it.

There is no particular method in that capacity, just rules to consider.

The most significant rule is to ensure you are both present. At this very moment. So as to do that, it's astute to take advantage of exotic nature rather than sexuality. This implies delicate contacts. Stroking regions in your body that don't excessively energize or manufacture sexual pressure. Getting a charge out of embraces and delicate kisses.

Tune down the energy and turn up a quiet, fun loving demeanour.

Try not to stress over climaxes — hers or yours — and make association and love the zenith of your closeness. Infiltration can be incorporated as long as you are both ready to continue the profundity of the association. Which is the reason you'll need to keep it very slow. Almost still. No pushing.

Simply being inside your lady. Try not to stress over keeping up your erection, as well. In the event that it leaves, keep making the most of your careful meeting without it. Whatever sort of touch you pick, take a gander at your accomplice's eyes. Check whether she is still with you or in the event that she wishes to be elsewhere.

Ask her questions - "What would i be able to do so you remain with us, presently?" The amount Mindful Sex to apply in your life. The real methodology will change a piece, contingent upon the phase of sexual separate that is as of now appearing in your lives. On the off chance that you are still generally partaking in your sexual coexistence together, the recommendation is to present careful sex sometimes on your traditional sex meetings.

If you notice that your companion is at a space where she's not completely with you explicitly, in the event that she stays away from sex or rejects your advances, I would suggest having just careful sex until things improve essentially.

Also, if your relationship is now at the sexless-marriage end of the scale, the mystery is to totally prematurely end any touch that your accomplice will decipher as something that would prompt sex. In the event that that is the place you are at your relationship; you will most likely need more assistance than basically perusing an article. Seeing a couples' specialist or a sexologist will be proper.

If you need to keep your partner explicitly fulfilled, first and foremost, ensure she can remain present while having intercourse. As it were at that point apply any method that turns you both on.

Most Stupidly Satisfying Things All Women Want in Bed

While sexual inclinations are distinctive for everybody, there are yet a scarcely any general precepts that have sex surprisingly better. Regardless of whether you have been with your accomplices for a very long time, or it's your first time having intercourse, here are 13 things all ladies need in bed.

1. Cunnilingus comparable to each other's sensual caress dream. You know how guys need you to be so into sucking their dick that you are like, choking and destroying? We need the equivalent for when we get head.

No, you do not need to destroy the yet enthusiastic energy, give her the blow job as well, it never hurt anybody.

2. Capacity to peruse the room: snuggling. Now and then you need to be snuggled and spooned, now and then you need to remain on inverse sides of the bed. While these inclinations can vary not just from individual to-individual, yet additionally with every circumstance, it's ideal to check in with your partner and see what's up. Only a straightforward "Would i be able to spoon you?" or then again something works here.

3. A receptive mind. Possibly you need to bring toys in with the general mish-mash or attempt something else in bed. Being powerless when you're stripped is even harder, so having an accomplice who you can trust and have a sense of security around is a key point.

4. Vocal energy. There is nothing more smoking than an accomplice who is just fed to be with you and cannot quit geeing out over how hot he thinks you are, or the amount you turn him on. Get boisterous and get freaky with it. Disclose to her the amount you need her and cannot quit considering her.

5. A partner contribute to my pleasure as well. A lady is not your hand, a substance light, or some other masturbatory help. Do not simply utilize her body till you climax

and afterward turn over and expect she made some extraordinary memories as well, since that is not how it functions.

Being a decent accomplice is about investing equivalent exertion. You would prefer not to be the individual who abandoned the gathering venture all semester, just to dip in and assume acknowledgment for the 'A' toward the end.

6. True serenity with regards to security. Be arranged, and expect we are doing it with a condom except if in any case settled upon heretofore. Try not to constrain me to take it off part of the way through or take a gander at me astounded with your dick hanging out of your jeans like you have never heard "condom" previously. Simply don't do it! I will exit. I truly will.

7. A climax. Sex should not end with simply the male climax — particularly if she has not had one yet. In case you will be excessively depleted after

you climax, ensure she's dealt with already. It's not rocket science. On the off chance that you know, without a doubt, you will get yours, would not you need your accomplice to have a ball as well?

8. Correspondence. There is a period and a spot for silently snort sex yet having an accomplice who inquires as to whether you're into something or in the event that you need it another way is likewise pleasant. You do not get any additional focuses for making it to the end goal without saying a peep.

9. A spotless bed. It's outrageously difficult to release yourself and appreciate yourself in the event that you can feel your calves catching up on against any sedimentary layers of sweat, grime, and hook-ups past on his Target sofa with each snort.

10. An extra telephone charger. In the event that I need to call a Uber a short time later, I need to have the option to tune in to music

or check Twitter on my ride back, what is more, I can't do that on the off chance that I idiotically let my telephone simply spoil for the nine what is more, a half minutes we engaged in sexual relations. What's more, in case I'm remaining the night, I may still need to check Twitter on the off chance that you nod off before me.

11. Foreplay. It is anything but a race to the end goal! You can take your

time and coax stuff out and have a good time. A little persistence will

convey you a long, long way. In addition if the climax was the main thing

that made a difference about sex, I'd date the USB block that charges my

vibrator.

12. Sock expulsion. If it's not too much trouble, please take off your socks before sex. It is just so abnormal to see somebody like, completely stripped yet at the same time wearing socks that it can truly remove you from the occasion.

In addition, at that point you run into the strange thing of like, "Should I have left my socks on?" "Do they dislike feet?" "Do they think my feet are appalling?!" and spiralling into a gap of foot-based tension, which isn't a spot anyone gets a kick out of the chance to be.

13. Practical desires. Kindly don't move into bed with me just to transform from Jake in Accounting to Ron Jeremy. Pornography sex is cool and all, however genuine sex isn't generally similar to that, and I despise the thought that it is absolutely typical for a person to flip you over silently and attempt to stick it in your rear end while considering you a messy skank and letting you know he is going to complete in your hair. Quit acting like your convertible 2-bed is a sex prisons

Attributes of Female Sexual Satisfaction

The significance of sexual fulfilment in a sound sentimental relationship is clear. It will in general be related with more significant levels of love, duty, and steadiness in the relationship and a lower separate from rate. Shockingly, sexual issues, likewise called sexual dysfunctions are genuinely normal. Research shows that in the United States, anyplace from about 10%-half of men, and 25%-60% of ladies experience the ill effects of some type of sexual brokenness, generally as low enthusiasm for sex or trouble accomplishing climax.

Age, physical, and enthusiastic wellbeing are critical factors in sexual

fulfilment versus brokenness. Men will in general have increasingly erectile

brokenness as they get more seasoned, while ladies will in general appreciate improved sexual working with age as long as oil isn't an issue.

In any case, given the job of estrogen in grease and its diminishing levels in ladies after menopause, grease can in all likelihood be a issue if not tended to. Another case of the conceivable job of hormones in female sexual fulfilment is the normal lessening in excitement that happens during the primary trimester of pregnancy, with recuperation as a rule during the last two trimesters.

Sexual Satisfaction by Population. Grown-ups who are hitched or in an in any case serious relationship tend to work better explicitly contrasted with their unattached partners, what is more, those with higher instructive achievement will in general have a superior sex life contrasted with grown-ups who accomplish less instructively. While race and ethnicity will in general have little relationship with the general pace of sexual brokenness, there is by all accounts some changeability in the sort of brokenness dependent on this segment.

For instance, African-American ladies will in general have less sexual desire contrasted with Hispanic and Caucasian ladies, while

Caucasian ladies appear to encounter more physical torment during sex.

Educational encounters, such as being the survivor of physical or sexual injury, will in general reduction sexual working in ladies, while having more than five lifetime sexual accomplices or having same-sex sexual accomplices do not.

While having conventional sex jobs in a marriage will in general be related with engaging in sexual relations all the more frequently, the degree of fulfilment in those relationships has not been altogether contemplated

Variables Associated With Higher Sexual Satisfaction in Women

Various components impact sexual fulfilment in ladies. While age can to some degree neutralize it, high sexual want and fulfilment with work and with the sentimental relationship a lady is in all advance sexual fulfilment. Explicitly fulfilled ladies will in general have levels of sexual want that are firmly coordinated with those of their accomplice.

There is some proof that while penis length doesn't will in general be a factor for sexual fulfilment, penis width might just be. Ladies who self-invigorate are additionally bound to feel explicitly fulfilled.

The hypothesis there is that ladies who self-invigorate are progressively mindful of their sexual needs and needs.

Correspondence, both for the most part and about one's sexual needs, is thought to be the most grounded factor in accomplishing sexual fulfilment. Ladies who will in general be profoundly explicitly emphatic will in general have more elevated levels of want, climax capacity, and sexual fulfilment contrasted with their non-assertive partners.

The more regularly couples will in general be friendly, both explicitly and something else, the higher their sexual fulfilment will in general be. Strikingly, even the type of correspondence can affect sexual fulfilment.

For instance, nonverbal correspondence during sex is believed to be almost certain related with sexual fulfilment than verbal correspondence during sex.

Given the significance of sexual fulfilment in keeping up wellbeing and bliss, just as the various variables engaged with female sexual fulfilment, ladies and their accomplices would be all around encouraged to secure their enthusiastic and physical wellbeing, be warm taking all things together parts of their relationship, become acquainted with their sexual needs, and impart those requirements straightforwardly and generous to their accomplices.

The Most Effective Method To Please A Man In Bed (Step By Step Guide)

This bit by bit control will not be some standard sexual intimacy talk.

It will start your creative mind, give you a few pointers, and get you to open up progressively about tricky subjects like satisfying a man in bed.

It will likewise show how impression of ourselves and our sexual wants

impact our closeness. This section will likewise give some succulent tips on the most proficient method to satisfy a man in bed bit by bit and, even more critically, how to draw the best for yourself and accomplish the most noteworthy sexual fulfilment.

Great sex is about common fulfilment. That is the reason you

ought to never overlook your sentiments and wants.

A great number of ladies dismisses their own wants. They put their own

delight second and sooner or later, it's unavoidable that a few issues emerge in bed.

Recall that your partner – giving that he is the best person for you – needs you to have fun as much as he does and significantly more.

The most ideal approach to learn is by approaching it slowly and carefully, so how about we start.

1. Quit overthinking things and transmit certainty. It is anything but a mystery that certainty is ridiculously hot. It emits the vibe that you are OK with what your identity is and you recognize what you need.

Obviously, we have our little instabilities. Be that as it may, you should never carry them to the room with you, so be cautious to abstain from committing that error.

The room (or any place else you chose to engage in sexual relations) is not the place where you ought to have any questions

about what you look like or how you
perform explicitly.

On the off chance that a man is going to
have intercourse with you, this is on the
grounds that he discovers you incredibly
alluring, and he has a faux pas the size of
Alaska to demonstrate it. So away with the
questions and in with the sex games.

What keeps us away from having and
conceding our accomplice an astounding
sexual experience is really our heads.

That is the reason we should ensure we
acknowledge ourselves and our bodies just
the way they are.

Likewise, we should remember that things
we consider blemished may be immaculate
to our accomplice or he probably will not
notice them. about his blemishes.

Furthermore, is managing them in his own
particular manner. Not that I'm a sex master,
be that as it may, for my situation, a little
recognition from you will assuredly help.

When we acknowledge our bodies with the ideal defects, it will think about us and our accomplice will get on the attractive vibes we send.

Likewise, you will have no issue leaving the lights on during sex, being

on top, strolling bare around the loft… or in any event, attempting wrinkles you never figured you would.

2. Everything starts in your brains - excellent lady remaining with man and taking a gander at camera.

When you are agreeable in your own body, it's the ideal opportunity for stage 2 – shining your partner's creative mind.

Before exercises between the sheets start, the genuine move is making

place in our brains.

By lighting the fire in our partner's creative mind and presumably in the

zone of his groin, we will all the while become horny ourselves.

There are a couple of manners by which we can do that: Sexting

Sexting is one of the first and best thoughts that come to mind. There are numerous bearings where sexting can go. It can change from inconspicuous vanilla messy converse with something no-nonsense.

It relies upon your inclinations, so let that be your rule. In any case, sexts will undoubtedly knock his socks off an In any case, sexts will undoubtedly take his breath away and make him anxious to see you also, remove your garments from you.

One of the incredible advantages of sexting is that you have a lot of time to consider what you are going to state.

Playing blended in with sexual ramifications appealing lady murmuring on keeps an eye on ear .

There are such many manners by which you
can tease to make your partner

want you more.

Words are incredible assets, so murmuring
something unusual in his ear,

posing grimy inquiries, saying something
before others that just he will comprehend in
a sexual way (some code name for
something sexual just you two know), and
furthermore utilizing body language can do
some incredible things when being a tease is
included.

Sending provocative photographs

Furthermore, no, do not send nudes. That is
never a smart thought since nudes can end
up everywhere throughout the web, so that
even the individuals who they were not
proposed for, wind up observing them.

Regardless of the amount you confide in your accomplice, one never realizes what the future may bring.

Along these lines, when sending provocative photographs or attractive snapchats, make it inconspicuous.

For example, you can send your cleavage (your boobs securely took care of

a ribbon bra), take a mirror selfie in attractive jeans, something along these

lines.

The thought is to touch off his creative mind, not to uncover all. All things considered; he is the person who needs to help uncover you.

3. Foreplay is everything - joined with the past advance is something that will drive your man insane. It resembles a prologue to the genuine intercourse, which can be similarly as charming.

The whole idea of foreplay is to suppress expectation and make the genuine sexual act substantially more energizing.

You needed to realize how to satisfy a man in bed bit by bit – foreplay

is the key that opens the ways to delight.

To begin it off, a great full body knead is something your partner is

sure, to appreciate.

Move slowly, turn some affection making music on, put some back rub oil on your hands, and let your fingers slide exotically all over his body.

On the off chance that you bother him by kneading his internal thighs, he will soften in your grasp.

Provocative underwear

This relies upon the man you are dating. Some appreciate provocative underwear so much that they will be turned on just by taking a gander at it or contacting it.

They will most likely request that you leave
it on during foreplay and during

sex (if it's conceivable).

Then again, there are men that could not
care less much about underwear –

they just incline toward rip your garments
off without giving it much thought, thinking
increasingly about what you have
underneath the layers.

Provocative underwear can likewise be
useful to you. It can cause you to feel
attractive also, certain, and that is
unquestionably something your accomplice
will pick up on and appreciate.

It is something that can be useful for couples
in long haul connections that are trapped in
an endless cycle and need to discover
approaches to flavour up their sexual
coexistence, yet in addition for new couples
who are into pretending.

Taking on another character in the room is
something that adds to the

newness and fun of your personal life.

A few jobs that couples normally prefer to carry on are teacher and understudy, repairman and mortgage holder, outsiders in a bar, pornography stars, team promoter and football player, prevailing and agreeable, and the rundown is perpetual.

The significant thing is to pick a sexual dream you are both alright with.

Kissing

There is nothing like kissing while participating in foreplay. Beginning with the lips is a decision where you cannot turn out badly.

Divert your kisses to his neck and remain there for some time.

At that point gradually snack his ear, returning to the neck and finding your

path down. Kiss every trace of his body.

Expectation of a sensual caress will be something that will make his masculinity hard as wood.

You can likewise change the power of your kisses. Contingent upon the state of mind, you can go from delayed to possessive, perhaps incorporate inconspicuous lip snacking.

The delicate quality of your lips on his body will give him goose bumps all over. Kissing is frequently underestimated, although it truly shouldn't be, as it can do ponders.

There is nothing that shouts stunning foreplay (to the extent most men are worried) as oral sex.

A blow job is something men appreciate as much as sex – or maybe even more. The tip of his penis is the most touchy part, that is the reason it needs extraordinary consideration.

Something that will make his experience much more noteworthy is on the off chance that you keep tenderly contacting his gonads. You can suck and kiss them as well.

It will give him more prominent delight than he would ever have longed for.

69 - The sex position "69" is something that will without a doubt incite

shared delight. 69ing includes 2 individuals performing oral sex on each other.

Hearing each other groan and grip from delight will make you both stimulated past cut off points.

Shared masturbation

This is additionally a decent foreplay strategy that will ensure the fulfilment of the two gatherings.

You will both have the option to see each other's countenances in joy and hear the groaning sounds that move in pitch.

At the point when faculties of sight and hearing are joined with the impression of delight that you incite in one another by utilizing hand developments, the feeling for both of you will be so noteworthy, there aren't sufficient words to clarify it.

Keep in mind, he needs you to have a good time as much as he does.

His capacity to fulfil you in bed is a significant turn on just as theverification of his great execution that he's been searching for.

Initiate sex

Men like ladies who are in contact with their sexuality. Thus, he will be more than glad if you start the moves that bit by bit lead to sex. You starting sex will cause him to feel needed.

Be direct, however go slowly. For example, you can put your hand on

his leg and stir your way up to his apparatus, request that he go along with you, at that point grasp his hand and guide it to your butt or boobs.

He will take it from that point – or just lead him to the room and start kissing him. There are a great deal of alternatives to utilize your creative mind and you will without a doubt shake his.

4. Game time

After you passed a few or the entirety of the previously mentioned ventures above, you are currently at the progression that you've been going for up and down: the real demonstration of engaging in sexual relations.

For the most part, this progression comes immediately with no compelling reason to over analyse or then again overthink it.

In any case, now and again, after moving your situations through and through, you'd like to include a little flavour. That is the place every single diverse sort of sex positions work mystically.

Along these lines, we should look at probably the most intriguing ones:

On top

As I previously stated, satisfying you is something strongly invigorating for your man.

With you on top, he'll have front seat see in seeing your joy direct. He will have the option to take in your whole body. Be that as it may he will most likely do significantly more than appreciate your body.

He may grab your abdomen or stroke your boobs while you are on him. This position is one of the urgent strides in this step by step manual to please your man in bed.

This position is additionally incredible for you since it gives you control, you direct the pace, and you can see exactly how you're causing him to ask for a greater amount of you.

Missionary position

The missionary position is essential and most couples start off with this

position. It gives the man the prevailing position.

Be that as it may, it likewise empowers delayed eye to eye connection and a great deal of kissing, and in doing as such, forms a superior association. The evangelist position is not one that ought to be disregarded.

Be that as it may, on the off chance that you need to get more from it, fold your legs over his abdomen and lock them on his back. You will draw him towards you, making the infiltration more profound.

On the other hand, putting your legs on his shoulders to frame a "V" shape will have a similar impact.

While he is on you, you can run your fingers through his hair, hold or stroke his arms, or get his back, making a joy actuated engraving of your fingers on his skin..

Those unobtrusive moves will tell him that you are having fun furthermore, that in the event that he props it up, you will come extremely hard actually soon – that will be all he needs to continue.

The missionary position is increasingly pleasurable for him since he gets to see your face making motions of fulfilment.

He will see your lips enlarge as you groan and tremble out of unadulterated joy. Realizing that it's all a result of him will make him incredibly cheerful both all through bed.

The seat

This position requests female control so don't be hesitant to assume responsibility.

The man, for this situation, speaks to the seat so to speak.

He is sitting with his legs outstretched before him, utilizing his hands as help.

The lady is on her male cooperate with her back to him, inclining close to his body.

You sit on him, clutching his hips, and lean your head marginally back while gradually going here and there.

Spooning

It resembles nestling and having intercourse
at the same time, which builds your level of
closeness. Your accomplice needs to rests
behind you and enter you delicately.

This position awards him full access to your
body. His hands can go all over you and it is
an ideal situation to exhibit his warmth also,
veneration for you.

While in this position, you can utilize your
hands and tenderly touch his body, pulling
him closer.

You can likewise contact yourself to
upgrade your pleasure – and his, as well,
since when he sees that you are jerking off
before him, it will make him crazy for you.

Sex before the mirror

It is time you begin glancing in the mirror in
an entire distinctive way.

If you and your accomplice choose to have
intercourse before a mirror, you will
presumably do it standing up, with your

hands pushed on the divider on the two sides
of the mirror.

With both you reflect confronting, twist
marginally so he can infiltrate you.

Hold your head up so he can see your
outward appearances and the level

of your satisfaction. He will likewise have a
mirror perspective on your front body parts
while he has the ideal perspective on your
base part.

For him, the mirror does some amazing
things. Then again, you aren't disregarded
here either in light of the fact that you can
likewise observe him, feel and see his hands
on your hips, and all things considered,
appreciate extraordinary sex.

Sex in the shower

Above all else, the shower is an
extraordinary spot for warming things up.
You can begin by taking a wipe or basically
utilize your hands to rub and wash his back.

Begin advancing down to his instrument, and remain for some time in that zone, while kissing his newly showered back.

While waiting in that position, give him a hand-work. It will both astound and stun him.

He will presumably not anticipate it – perhaps he is never had anyone contact his masculinity from that point – with the exception of himself, clearly.

The remainder of the shower exercises will develop all alone. Let him

make the following move. You'll most likely engage in sexual relations standing up, with not just pieces of your body wet, yet your whole body.

Fast in and out

A fast in and out isn't something you plan. It's something that occurs. So

at the point when you feel the desire, simply let yourself proceed to appreciate it. Your man will value your feeling of experience.

A fast in and out can happen whenever and anyplace. In any case, the primary driver for it is your shared deep longing that should be diminished.

Thus, do not get tied up with that gibberish that sex must be enduring to be significant.

A decent fast in and out every once in a while, does some amazing things. Here and there, you just have restricted time or maybe no longing for foreplay, so you simply skip directly past that progression.

In any case, a fast in and out will be all you both should be totally fulfilled for the remainder of the day.

Cowgirl

This is one more position that awards you full control. You direct the speed, profundity, edge, and force of the development.

It is the simplest method to hit your G-spot
and make you come everywhere your
partner.

The nuts and bolts of this position is that
you sit on your accomplice, turning your
back toward him, while he lies level on the
bed.

You can utilize his knees as help and
basically make developments that best fulfil
you both. This position is rawer than it is
close.

It does not give you eye to eye connection or
that sentiment of closeness. That does not
make it any less pleasurable. It gives him an
incredible view of your behind, and in the
event that he is an ass man, he will adore
this position.

In addition, you can generally glance back at
him for a second while you are riding him.
That quick look will toss both of you over
the top.

The pretzel

The name of this position is charming and something most likely new to the both of you. Fortunately, it is not as muddled as it sounds.

This position requests that you rest on your side. Leave your base leg extended and level.

He will ride your base leg while bowing down. Your other leg will be twisted around his abdomen.

This position empowers profound infiltration – like the one you would feel during doggy style – just this one empowers you that valuable eye contact.

The other advantage is that it leaves his hands allowed to do whatever he needs with them.

Doggy style

On the off chance that your accomplice loves your goods, this will be one of his top pick sex positions. To accomplish this position, you need to jump down on the ground.

He stoops, infiltrating you from behind with his body inclining toward yours.

This position awards him incredible fulfilment. He can appreciate the view from behind. He can snatch your abdomen or pull your hair if things get a bit harsher.

He additionally needs to work with you on finding a shared mood that will fulfil you both.

The level iron

Lie on your stomach with your legs level and your hips somewhat raised.

He will ride both of your legs and infiltrate
you bowing down.

This position gives him a more tightly
feeling that he and you find absolutely
pleasurable.

The level iron additionally furnishes you
with the sentiment of closeness and
closeness you lose during some other "back"
sex positions.

5. Ensure you praise his presentation - Men
love to be praised on their exhibitions. They
need you to make some incredible memories
with them; they need to satisfy you
explicitly.

A man needs to flourish at sex more than
some other piece of life.

Even though your activities during sex non-
verbally said that you adored

his moves and had fun, it is anything but a
poorly conceived notion to state it out loud.

So after sex, while you are lying in bed
snuggling, you may state something along

the lines of, "OMG that was incredible." or "What was that?! Wooow."

Basically express your real thoughts on how you feel at that time, however don't try too hard. Simply little inspirational statements are sufficient.

The commendations are not there just to help his sense of self. They are moreover there so he realizes that regardless of whether you haven't arrived at climax, you made some great memories.

As a rule, ladies need additional time than men to peak and that is something common.

In this way, don't overplay it. One of the following occasions you'll get there, so don't bring down his confidence by saying you weren't fulfilled.

6. Be mischievous and daring -The best, and presumably the main way you can bomb in

your endeavour to fulfils a man is in the
event that you don't do anything.

On the off chance that you simply lie level
on your back anticipating that him should do
everything.

That is not something that will make him
upbeat and fulfilled.

In any case, in case you're prepared to invest
in even the scarcest energy, your man is sure
to value it.

He needs to realize that you're really living
it up and not pondering what you will have
for lunch the following day.

All he needs is to feel needed. The most
ideal approach to accomplish that is by
being somewhat mischievous and daring.

And keeping in mind that he may like your
pleasantness and gentility outside the room,

inside the room, he would invite your base
desires rising.

Thus, start sex, snatch his butt, play with his
balls, nibble him on his neck let your
creative mind go crazy

. Unwind and have a good time.

Don't overthink the entire circumstance –
you'll just keep down the both of you.

In spite of the fact that your inquiry was the
way to satisfy a man in bed bit by bit, it's
essential to include that the bed shouldn't be
the main spot where

joys are satisfied.

Be brave. Search for new places to have
intercourse in or humour him in

a portion of his dreams.

So imagine a scenario in which you have a
loft, that doesn't imply that sex in the
rearward sitting arrangement of the vehicle
won't be only the thing you need.

You can likewise attempt a spot that
conveys a danger of being gotten – like

sex on the gallery with the risk that a portion
of your neighbours may

see you, or a fast in and out in a changing
room whenever you go garments shopping.

Be striking. Try not to let anything alarm
you. Benefit as much as possible from each
second you spend in bed – and outside of it.

The way to having incredible sex is having a
passionate bond, as well.

In the event that you coexist with your
accomplice in different parts of your life
together, your sexual coexistence will thrive
from it.

In such a case that you have both passionate
and physical bonds, there is no halting you.
The more you take part in sexual exercises,
the better the sex.

Like every single beneficial thing in life,sex
additionally improves with training.

You'll become more acquainted with your accomplice, his preferences, his dreams also, sexual wants – and he'll know yours.

At the point when you're both in it for the common delight, it can't beat that.

I simply need to pressure again the significance of trust in all of this. On the off chance that you let your uncertainties aside and live at the time,

you're now a large portion of the way.

Try not to let anything keep you down. By permitting yourself to feel OK with yourself, you'll consequently appreciate sex more than you at any point thought conceivable.

That is only the trigger your accomplice should be fulfilled in bed, as well. It's all straightforward when you take a gander at it.

He has to realize that you are satisfied so he can be satisfied, as well.

18 Things He's Secretly Dying for You to Try In Bed

What dazzles a person most in bed? Shockingly (or possibly not really, folks

do have gained notoriety for being apathetic), most admitted that they are definitely not all that intrigued by showy behaviour or trapeze acts. Truth be told, numerous men unveiled that they are basic animals who essentially simply need their spouses to appear. Be that as it may, in case you're hoping to give him something extra-extraordinary, they'd love a tad of this.

1. Do It With the Lights On

You might be stressed over what your better half thinks about your post-bosom taking care of boobs, your C-area scar, or that eventually, he'll quit being pulled in to you since you look a little — OK, a parcel— unique in relation to you did on your big day. In any case, men once in a while notice your self-saw defects — they possibly become mindful of them in case you're distracted with them or make a special effort to conceal. "It's actual, men are exceptionally visual, but it's extremely about needing to have the option to really observe you move, ideally with no garments on. We're approved by how glad we can make you in bed, and that is what we're cantered around—not on the amount you may have changed." So permit him see you. Every one of you.

2. Touch Yourself

A few ladies — and men — might locate this a humiliating, however hear me out. Viewing a certain lady completely interface with her sexuality is a gigantic turn-on for men,. It resembles giving your significant other a private peep appear, and having the option to see the delight all over and improve comprehension of precisely how you like to be contacted is both a turn-on and an important exercise.

3. Utilize Your Mouth

Call them Captain Obvious, yet actually men love landing blow positions, and they love it at the point when ladies take it upon themselves — no asking or asking required—to give one. So feel free to astound him, and not on the grounds that it's his birthday or you lost a wager.

4. Be Vocal

We are not proposing shockingly counterfeit pornography star-groans, however men need to realize when you're having a good time. That doesn't really mean you have to speak profanely, similar to 'f - me harder' — can make men freeze up.

Revealing to them when you like something—'I love it when you f - me hard'— is far superior." You may ponder the purpose of "oohs" and "ahhs" after such a long time — all things considered, he likely comprehends what works at this point. Be that as it may, on the off chance that you let yourself proceed to pant a minimal like bygone eras, you might be amazed by how he react to that approval — and what his recharged fervor will do to you.

5. Concentrate On His Sensitive Spots

The tip of his penis ought to be given extraordinary consideration, however realize that a flick of the tongue to a great extent will leave your man stunned.

6. Go anyplace But In Bed

Men fantasize about having intercourse in better places. While schedule

sex has its place, he here and there needs to accomplish something else—and that is beneficial for you as well. Basically ride him on the lounge chair while the children are at a sleepover — simply ensure the TV is killed behind you.

7. Slow Down

We have all been there: You're completely depleted and attempting to get it

done or you're just up to speed in what's going on and your body normally goes quick. Be that as it may, decelerating can be amazing. Men like being

ready to feel everything and to have the opportunity to investigate.

For instance, in case you're performing oral sex, take him right in also, out gradually so he's marginally contacting your mouth. Once

you're finished prodding him you can go max speed, however in the starting, a light method goes far.

8. Hotshot Your Acting Chops

Many wedded men stress they will get exhausted of having intercourse with

only one lady. That is the reason pretending is so viable. Notwithstanding having you — his spectacular spouse — your significant other can likewise get feisty with the "barista" or "servant." "Going into dream mode consequently builds levels of dopamine, the excitement hormone, and lifts your feeling of connection. So significantly after you're through getting down with the "cop" or "privateer," you'll feel nearer to one another for having accomplished something novel together.

9. Keep in mind the Power of Foreplay

Without a doubt, folks have gained notoriety for needing to get it on in no time, in any case, don't get overlook that the development can be similarly as hot. Regardless of whether it's an attractive book you send to get him energized or gradually undressing for an off the cuff a striptease, take a stab at getting him fired up before you even start. Why hurry to the headliner when you can develop to something much more blazing?

10. Let Him Dominate You

Couples so frequently get into a sex routine — same time of night, same

place, same position. And keeping in mind that your significant other may

not make a functioning move to change things, men need to have the ability to switch up examples and take all out control. Get out one of his silk ties, have him tie your hands together, and let him take it from there. We presume you will love it

11. Accomplish Something Taboo

The majority of the men we talked with trusted that they're keen on attempting — or having more — butt-centric sex. The nearly illegal nature of this demonstration and the weakness it requires from you make it something men truly need to understanding, however would prefer not to recommend out of dread of culpable you. On the off chance that you'd be ready for exploring different avenues regarding butt-centric and suspect your better half would appreciate it, start a discussion.

Not exactly prepared for butt-centric at this time? Attempt these nearly butt-centric positions.

12. Contact the Unexpected Places

Did you realize that men have a great deal of spots that can be erogenous-of places, other than the penis? There are semi-evident spots like a person's middle or inward musings, yet remember lesser-thought of attractive sports, similar to his sanctuaries or behind his knees.

13. Enjoy His Fantasy

Now and then, it just pays to inquire. Much the same as no two ladies are the equivalent, no two men are the equivalent — nor are their dreams. Ask your accomplice what his definitive hot wish is, and afterward enjoy precisely that.

Regardless of whether he's been kicking the bucket to see you in a particular sort of underwear or have you rule him, you'll possibly know whether you inquire. Accepting that you're in a solid, legitimate relationship, he'll be glad to open up.

14. Spruce Up

Never under any circumstance think little of the intensity of a transparent teddy to get your fellow standing tall. Anything that causes a lady to feel great in her body furthermore, explicitly certain is provocative.

Basically, nothing is hotter to your person than certainty. I can by and by bear witness to this reality; my man can't help it this provocative little (and I underline pretty much nothing) red nightie that a apathetically walk around in now and again.

Be that as it may, it's not even just wearing the undergarments. It's the bother, the hot content you send him telling him you got some undergarments however he needs to hold up until the evening. Take as much time as is needed and assume responsibility, on the grounds that the ball is in your court and your man needs it al.

15. Enjoy Some Prostate Play

The prostate may be a new area for you, or it may be new region for you and your person, or possibly he's been too modest to even think about asking for

a finger up his butt, yet don't leave the prostate unattended. It's time to show your person how much delight he is absent in his derrière.

A great deal of the penis is inner; it nearly resembles a boomerang. With secondary passage play, you're kneading these inward nerve endings and that can feel great. Start by including a finger when you're both exceptionally stirred.

Before sufficiently long, he'll be asking why he wasn't at that point exploring different avenues regarding prostate play. It's very worth testing those waters.

16. Grow Your Menu

It's simple for any couple to get in a sexual groove. What occurs in a relationship is all that you like and your accomplice like remains on the menu, yet anything both of you doesn't care for, isn't attempted, So make a rundown of yes/no/not for the present and after some time as you build up the closeness, the security, and the association, at that point you can be like 'alright, for what reason don't we return and visit pretend or return and return to butt-centric play. It's that basic!

Think about all the pleasant you'll have
working the rundown out together. (What's
more, how much simpler your sexual
coexistence will be the point at which you
two aren't scrambling to consider new sex
positions without giving it much thought.)

17. Fuse a Toy

Think sex toys are only for when you need
to get off performance? Reconsider — there
are a lot of sex toys out there that are
intended for both of you. You could likewise
give him a hot show and let him watch you
use your new most loved vibrator.

18. Speak profanely

This is your opportunity to get inventive.
There are a lot of too hot things ladies can
say to men in bed that will make the
experience

more sizzling for both of you. Since how
about we be genuine: There's not much

alluring than somebody who's open about
what she enjoys.

Signs He's Satisfied In Bed (And Wants You All The Damn Time

On the off chance that he is cheerful, you'll
know.

Sex has gotten an inexorably significant and
talked about piece of grown-upcouples'
lives, and that implies that it's extremely
regular for individuals towonder on the off
chance that they're satisfying their
accomplices in bed.

With all the insane stuff being posted on the web, it'sanything but difficult to feel like you're insufficient, regardless of whether you are. This is particularly obvious when most folks won't straightforwardly concede that they aren't feeling it in bed.

That being stated, the majority of us have thought about whether we're truly in the same class as our partner state we are. Here are ten signs that they aren't feigning.

1. He starts sex.

As a rule, a dead room or an uneven room is a sign that he's not being satisfied by you. On the off chance that anything, it proposes that you ought to most likely be investigating a separation. In the event that he's starting on a standard premise, he's despite everything appreciating getting it from you.

2. He's quite playful.

Accepting that you two are engaging in sexual relations and you're likewise explicitly upbeat, a person who appears to be glad in general is a decent sign. Men who aren't fulfilled will in general be testy, peevish, or inaccessible. They may likewise simply appear generally speaking discouraged.

3. Sex is certainly not a major issue in your relationship.

An extremely astute individual once brought up that sex is the main issue that is never a serious deal when it's agreeable, yet can be the potential issue when it's no more. On the off chance that it doesn't appear as though it's an issue to both of you, he's content with what he's getting.

4. Snuggling is normal.

Sex isn't just about P in V. It's about the whole experience, and folks won't be satisfied without some delicate strokes and kisses in the blend. Snuggles and different types of friendship are what makes sex with

your sentimental partner not the same as sex
he would have with a flash light.

That is the reason folks love.

5. He discloses to you he's fulfilled.

On the off chance that a person says he's
glad, he generally is. Folks are really
legitimate about things like that. Along these
lines, on the off chance that you have any
inquiry about how he feels, inquire him. As
a general rule, he'll reveal to you straight up
how he feels.

6. Oral sex is responded.

More often than not, a person who isn't
liking his sexual coexistence won't be oral.
The motivation behind why is on the
grounds that he will feel like he's giving,
however not getting, and that will make him
quit giving. On the off chance that he's
licking you up, it's a decent sign.

7. Friendship, by and large, is visit between
both of you.

An individual who isn't getting explicitly fulfilled will once in a while ever go out of their approach to be friendly with their accomplice. On the off chance that he's consistently kissing on you, it's a sign he cherishes you.

8. He isn't wandering.

Try not to misunderstand me: even fulfilled men can wander. However, on the off chance that a person remains faithful to you, it's frequently a sign that he's likewise content with the way things are sleeping.

9. You really try tuning in to what he needs in bed, keeping a receptive outlook, and being obliging to him.

A person who has a young lady ready to meet him midway generally will be very appreciative for it. It's in reality truly uncommon to have, and that is the reason

numerous men are quite glad to be with
somebody who offers them that.

10. He boasts about it.

In the event that he's extremely cheerful,
you may catch him boasting to his
companions about what an incredible sexual
coexistence he has. That implies you truly
are the lady he's everything about.